TURTLE POWER!

By Danielle Denega
Illustrated by Artful Doodlers

New York   London   Toronto   Sydney

Based on the film TMNT™ by Imagi Animation Studios and Warner Bros.

An imprint of Simon & Schuster Children's Publishing Division
1230 Avenue of the Americas, New York, NY 10020
© 2007 Mirage Studios, Inc. *Teenage Mutant Ninja Turtles*™ and TMNT
are trademarks of Mirage Studios, Inc. All rights reserved.

Turtle Tots

Before they became the Teenage Mutant Ninja Turtles,
the four brothers were regular baby turtles!
Draw the baby turtles in their aquarium.

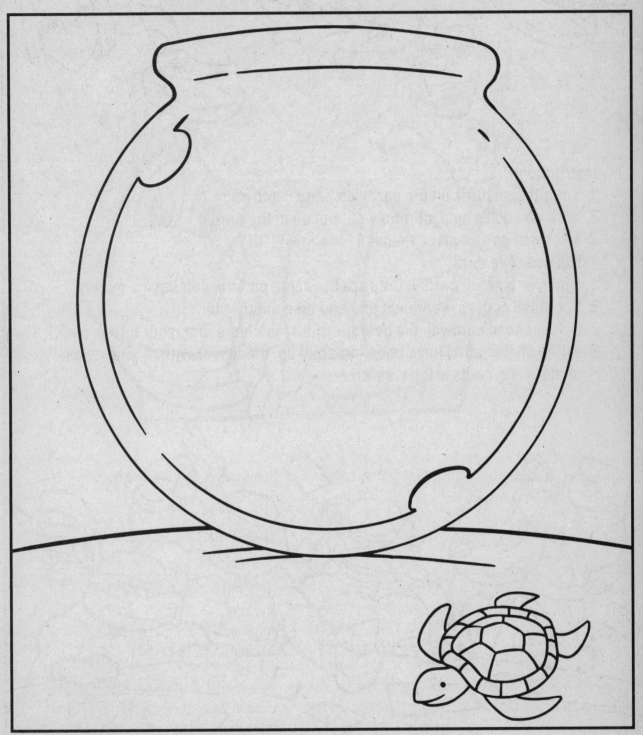

Ninja Memory Game

Instructions:

1. Color the pictures on the cards on page 5 and page 7.
2. With an adult's help, carefully cut out all of the cards.
3. Mix them up and place them all facedown.
4. Flip over one card.
5. Flip over another card. If they are the same picture, you have a match!
6. Put those cards in your own pile and take another turn.
7. If the second card you flip over does not match the first, your turn is over.
8. When all the cards have been matched up, the player with the most sets of matching cards is the winner!

MICHELANGELO   MICHELANGELO   SPLINTER   SPLINTER

RAPHAEL   RAPHAEL   CASEY   CASEY

APRIL   APRIL   DONATELLO   DONATELLO

LEONARDO   LEONARDO   MAXIMILLIAN   MAXIMILLIAN

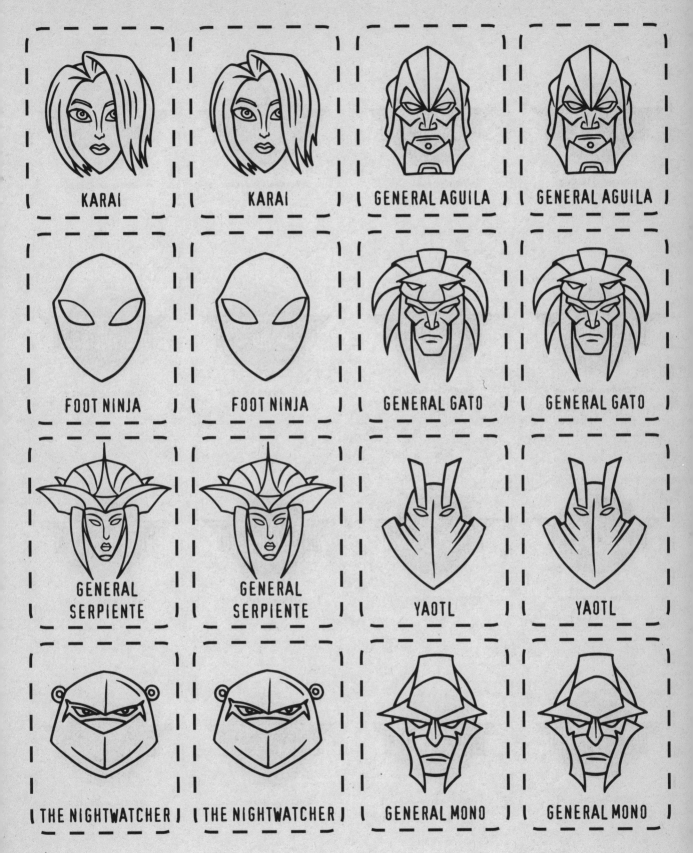

KARAI

KARAI

GENERAL AGUILA

GENERAL AGUILA

FOOT NINJA

FOOT NINJA

GENERAL GATO

GENERAL GATO

GENERAL SERPIENTE

GENERAL SERPIENTE

YAOTL

YAOTL

THE NIGHTWATCHER

THE NIGHTWATCHER

GENERAL MONO

GENERAL MONO

Find the Foot

Find and circle the two Foot Ninjas who look exactly the same.

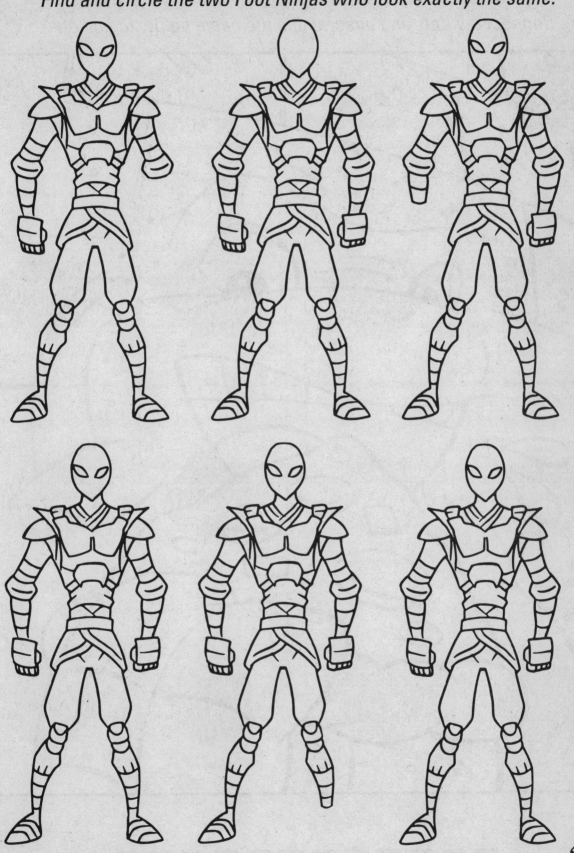

9

Who Is It?

Who's the most fun-loving Teenage Mutant Ninja Turtle?
Connect the dots and unscramble the name below to find out.

10

A I N C M G H E E L O L

Ninja Mask

Materials:
Crayons or markers
Scissors
Hole punch
Ribbon or yarn

Instructions:
1. Color in the mask on this page. You can make it match your favorite Turtle's mask!
2. With an adult's help, carefully cut out the mask along the dashed lines.
3. Punch out the circle at the end of each side of the mask.
4. Thread a piece of ribbon or yarn through the holes to fasten the mask around your head.

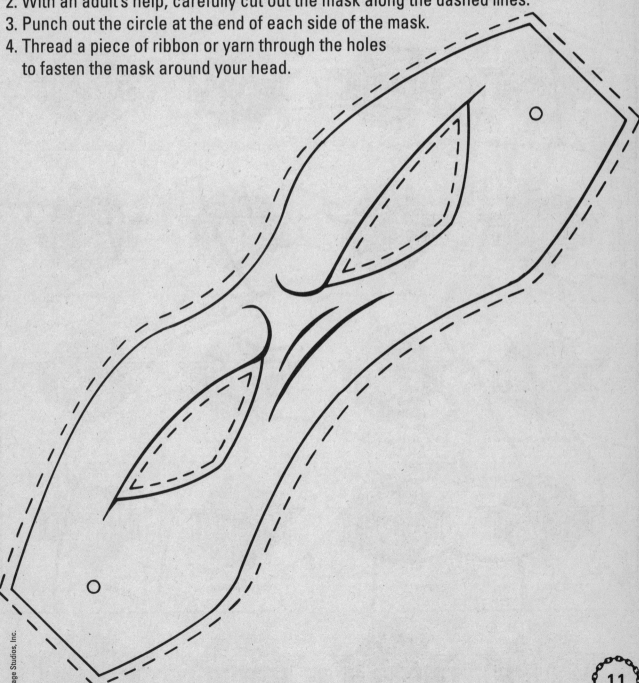

© 2007 Mirage Studios, Inc.

© 2007 Mirage Studios, Inc.

© 2007 Mirage Studios, Inc.

© 2007 Mirage Studios, Inc.

© 2007 Mirage Studios, Inc.

© 2007 Mirage Studios, Inc.

© 2007 Mirage Studios, Inc.

© 2007 Mirage Studios, Inc.

© 2007 Mirage Studios, Inc.

© 2007 Mirage Studios, Inc.

© 2007 Mirage Studios, Inc.

© 2007 Mirage Studios, Inc.

© 2007 Mirage Studios, Inc.

© 2007 Mirage Studios, Inc.

© 2007 Mirage Studios, Inc.

© 2007 Mirage Studios, Inc.

© 2007 Mirage Studios, Inc.

© 2007 Mirage Studios, Inc.

© 2007 Mirage Studios, Inc.

© 2007 Mirage Studios, Inc.

© 2007 Mirage Studios, Inc.

© 2007 Mirage Studios, Inc.

© 2007 Mirage Studios, Inc.

© 2007 Mirage Studios, Inc.

© 2007 Mirage Studios, Inc.

© 2007 Mirage Studios, Inc.

© 2007 Mirage Studios, Inc.

© 2007 Mirage Studios, Inc.

Word Search

Find and circle the words from the list below in any direction.

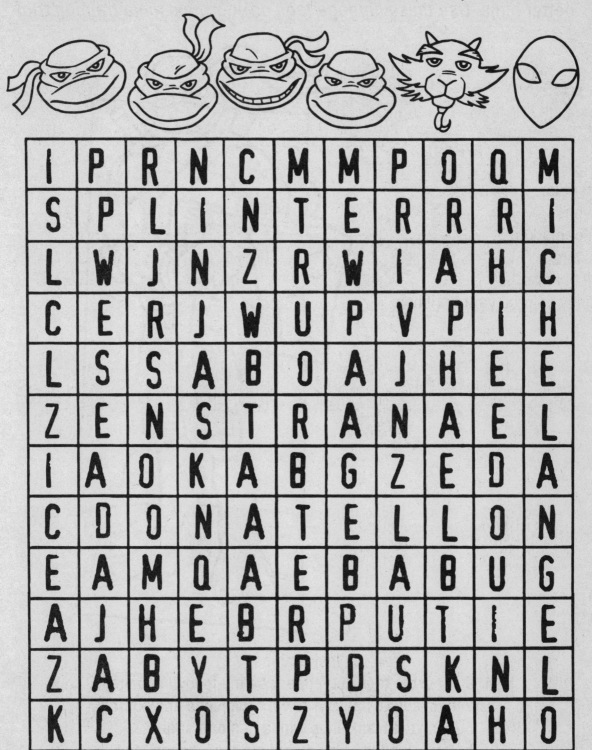

I	P	R	N	C	M	M	P	O	Q	M
S	P	L	I	N	T	E	R	R	R	I
L	W	J	N	Z	R	W	I	A	H	C
C	E	R	J	W	U	P	V	P	I	H
L	S	S	A	B	O	A	J	H	E	E
Z	E	N	S	T	R	A	N	A	E	L
I	A	O	K	A	B	G	Z	E	D	A
C	D	O	N	A	T	E	L	L	O	N
E	A	M	Q	A	E	B	A	B	U	G
A	J	H	E	B	R	P	U	T	I	E
Z	A	B	Y	T	P	D	S	K	N	L
K	C	X	O	S	Z	Y	O	A	H	O

RAPHAEL   **LEONARDO**

MICHELANGELO   **SPLINTER**

DONATELLO   **NINJAS**

Ninja Turtle Luggage Tags

Leonardo has been traveling the world, training to become an even better ninja. *Use these luggage tags on* your *next ninja training trip!*

Materials:
Crayons
Pen or marker
Scissors
Hole punch
Brightly colored yarn or ribbon

Instructions:
1. Color in the tags that appear on the following pages.
2. With an adult's help, write your full name and address on the blank lines with a pen or marker.
3. Have an adult help you cut out the luggage tags.
4. Punch a hole on the side of each tag where the circle is.
5. Fasten these tags to your bags or suitcases using brightly colored yarn or ribbon.

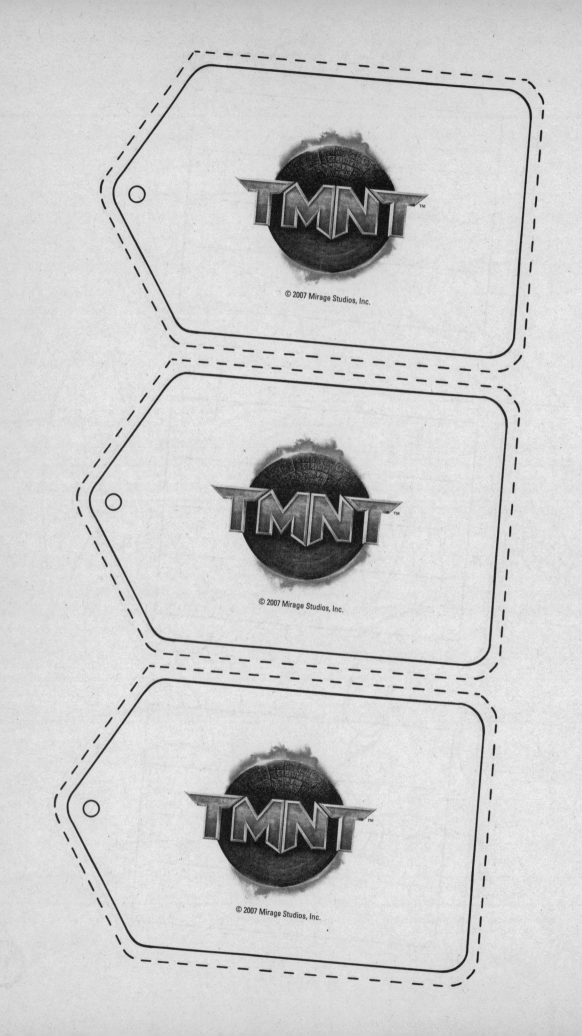

© 2007 Mirage Studios, Inc.

© 2007 Mirage Studios, Inc.

© 2007 Mirage Studios, Inc.

Color by Number

Color in the scene by following the code below.

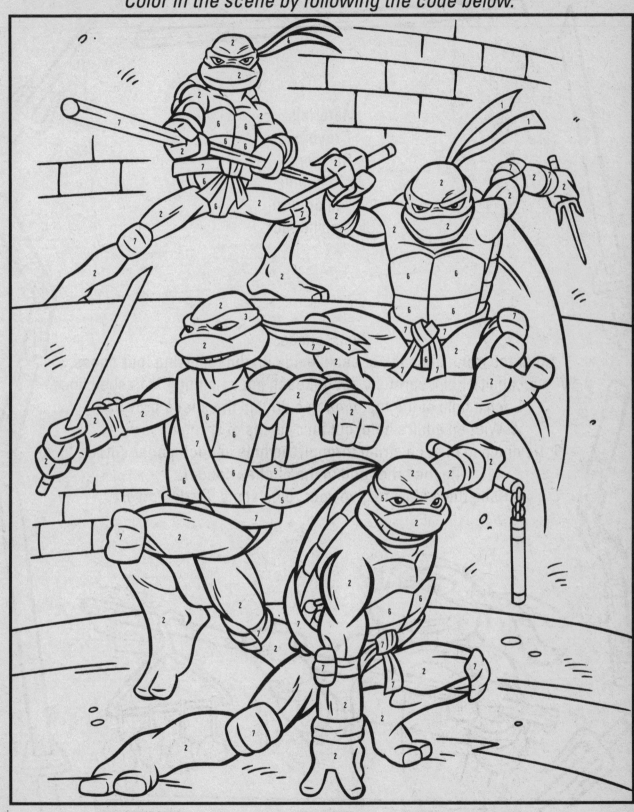

1 = RED   4 = PURPLE   7 = BROWN
2 = GREEN   5 = ORANGE
3 = BLUE   6 = YELLOW

Ninja Turtle Mobile

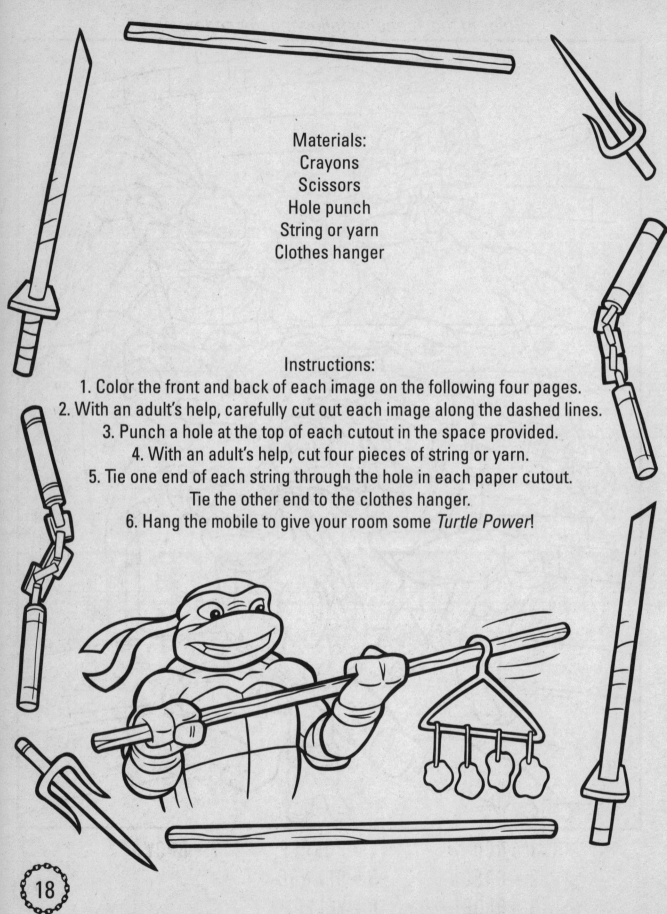

Materials:
Crayons
Scissors
Hole punch
String or yarn
Clothes hanger

Instructions:
1. Color the front and back of each image on the following four pages.
2. With an adult's help, carefully cut out each image along the dashed lines.
3. Punch a hole at the top of each cutout in the space provided.
4. With an adult's help, cut four pieces of string or yarn.
5. Tie one end of each string through the hole in each paper cutout. Tie the other end to the clothes hanger.
6. Hang the mobile to give your room some *Turtle Power*!

© 2007 Mirage Studios, Inc.

© 2007 Mirage Studios, Inc.

Casey Cleanup

Casey's apartment is a mess! *Help him clean up by circling all the sports equipment you see in the image below.*

Ninja Family

Splinter says, "The answer that lies in all our questions is . . . family."
Follow the instructions below to show your own family unity.

Materials:
Pencils
Construction paper
Scissors
Markers
Crayons
Glue

Instructions:
1. Have all of your family members trace
one of their hands on pieces of construction paper.
2. With an adult's help, carefully cut out the handprints.
3. Have your family members print their names on their handprints.
Each person can also draw a picture, write a sentence about families,
or decorate their handprint with paint, crayons, or stickers.
4. Glue the handprints together in a circle, with the fingers
pointing out, to make a family wreath!

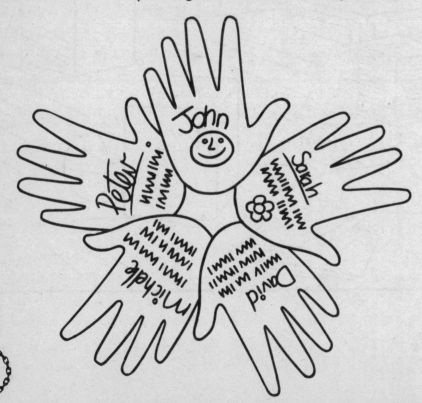

The Name Game

Fill in the blanks below to complete the characters' names.

1. _ _ _ _ I _

2. _ _ _ S _ _

3. S _ _ _ _ _ _ _ _ _ _ _

4. _ A _ _ _ _

25

Weapon Matchup

Draw a line to match each Turtle with his favorite weapon.

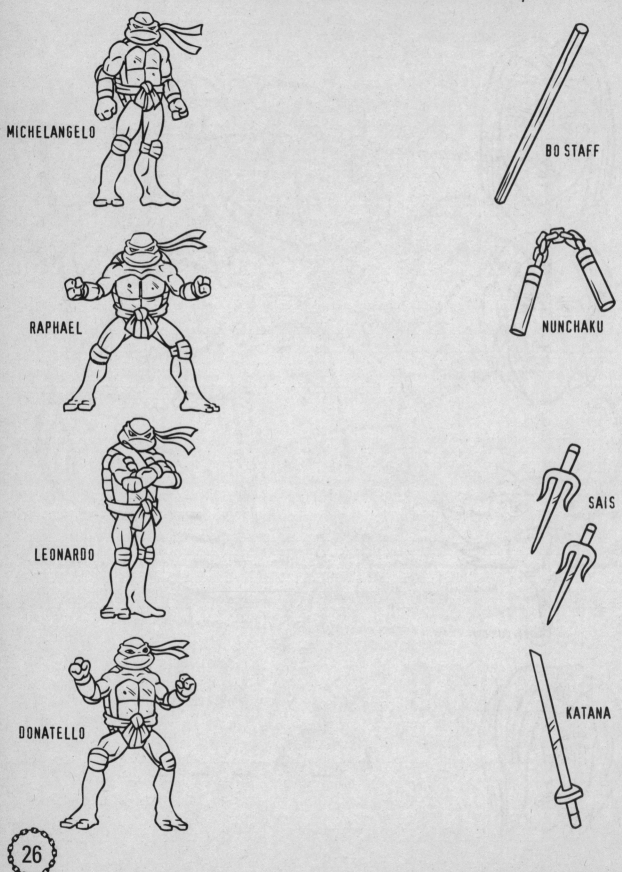

MICHELANGELO

RAPHAEL

LEONARDO

DONATELLO

BO STAFF

NUNCHAKU

SAIS

KATANA

Michelangelo's Magic Mirror

Hold this page up to a mirror to reveal Michelangelo's message.

COWABUNGA, DUDES!

Origami Turtle

Follow the instructions below to create a paper turtle.

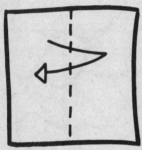

1. Using a square piece of paper, fold it side to side and then unfold.

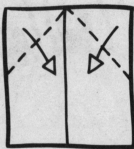

2. Turn it over and fold the right and left points down.

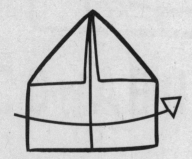

3. Flip the paper over.

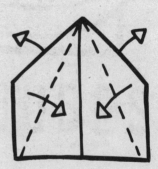

4. Bring the folded edges to meet the center fold, allowing the side points underneath to pop out.

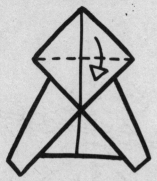

5. Fold the top point down as shown.

6. Fold the point upward to create the turtle's head.

7. Lift the bottom edge to meet the vertical center line.

8. Press flat and then fold outward as shown.

9. Repeat steps 7 and 8 with the other foot.

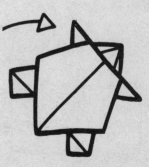

10. Turn it over and you have a turtle! Decorate it with stickers, crayons, or markers.

Super Scenery

Draw an exciting scene around the Turtles.

Donatello's Puzzle

Donatello is always putting new inventions together. *Put together your own puzzle by following the instructions below.*

Instructions:
1. Color in the picture below.
2. With an adult's help, carefully cut out the squares along the dashed lines to make puzzle pieces.
3. Mix up the pieces and then put the puzzle back together again!

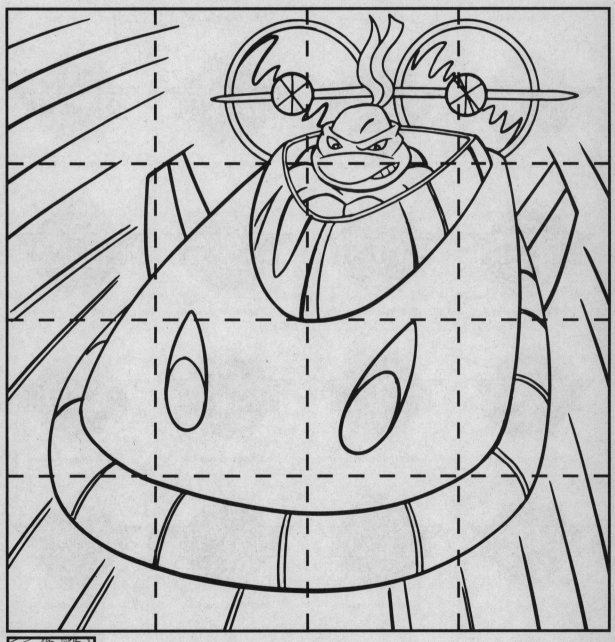

© 2007 Mirage Studios, Inc.   © 2007 Mirage Studios, Inc.   © 2007 Mirage Studios, Inc.   © 2007 Mirage Studios, Inc.

© 2007 Mirage Studios, Inc.   © 2007 Mirage Studios, Inc.   © 2007 Mirage Studios, Inc.   © 2007 Mirage Studios, Inc.

© 2007 Mirage Studios, Inc.   © 2007 Mirage Studios, Inc.   © 2007 Mirage Studios, Inc.   © 2007 Mirage Studios, Inc.

© 2007 Mirage Studios, Inc.   © 2007 Mirage Studios, Inc.   © 2007 Mirage Studios, Inc.   © 2007 Mirage Studios, Inc.

© 2007 Mirage Studios, Inc.   © 2007 Mirage Studios, Inc.   © 2007 Mirage Studios, Inc.   © 2007 Mirage Studios, Inc.

© 2007 Mirage Studios, Inc.   © 2007 Mirage Studios, Inc.   © 2007 Mirage Studios, Inc.   © 2007 Mirage Studios, Inc.

© 2007 Mirage Studios, Inc.   © 2007 Mirage Studios, Inc.   © 2007 Mirage Studios, Inc.   © 2007 Mirage Studios, Inc.

Monster Mash

Use crayons, markers, or stickers to put the captured monsters in their cells.

Catch a Criminal

Follow the maze to help the Nightwatcher capture the criminal.

START

FINISH

Turtle Time Doorknob Hanger

Every Turtle needs some privacy once in a while. *Follow the instructions to make your own doorknob hanger!*

Materials:
Crayons or markers
Scissors

Instructions:
1. Color in the doorknob hanger on this page and the next.
2. With an adult's help, carefully cut out the hanger along the dashed lines.
3. Hang it on your doorknob for everyone to see.

Ninja Code

Break this ninja code to help the Turtles save New York City!
*Write the letter that matches each number on the lines
below to reveal an important message.*

19 18 1 13 10 9 11   18 11

_ _ _ _ _ _ _   _ _

23 2 3 13 24

_ _ _ _ _ !

NINJA CODE KEY:

2	4	6	8	10	12	14	16	18	20	22	24	26	1	3	5	7	9	11	13	15	17	19	21	23	25
A	B	C	D	E	F	G	H	I	J	K	L	M	N	O	P	Q	R	S	T	U	V	W	X	Y	Z

Ninja Crossword

Use the clues below to fill in the crossword puzzle.

ACROSS
1. THE TEENAGE MUTANT NINJA
   TURTLES' MASTER
2. THE TURTLES' BEST HUMAN FRIEND

DOWN
3. RAPHAEL'S WEAPONS OF CHOICE
4. GLOBAL NINJA CRIME ORGANIZATION
5. MICHELANGELO'S FAVORITE FOOD

Turtle World

Create a world for the Turtles to explore.

Materials:
Shoe box
Crayons, markers, or paint
Construction paper
Scissors

Instructions:
1. Take the bottom part of a shoe box.
2. Decorate the inside of the box with buildings, jungles, deserts, or any other landscape you can think of. Try using crayons, markers, paint, or construction paper.
3. Turn the box so that the opening faces you.
4. Color in the characters, then with an adult's help, cut them out along the dashed lines.
5. Fold the flap on the bottom of each character along the solid line to make him stand up.
6. Place the characters inside the shoe box, then have them explore the world you created!

© 2007 Mirage Studios, Inc.

© 2007 Mirage Studios, Inc.

© 2007 Mirage Studios, Inc.

© 2007 Mirage Studios, Inc.

© 2007 Mirage Studios, Inc.

© 2007 Mirage Studios, Inc.

© 2007 Mirage Studios, Inc.

© 2007 Mirage Studios, Inc.

© 2007 Mirage Studios, Inc.

© 2007 Mirage Studios, Inc.

© 2007 Mirage Studios, Inc.

© 2007 Mirage Studios, Inc.

© 2007 Mirage Studios, Inc.

© 2007 Mirage Studios, Inc.

© 2007 Mirage Studios, Inc.

© 2007 Mirage Studios, Inc.

© 2007 Mirage Studios, Inc.

© 2007 Mirage Studios, Inc.

© 2007 Mirage Studios, Inc.

© 2007 Mirage Studios, Inc.

© 2007 Mirage Studios, Inc.

© 2007 Mirage Studios, Inc.

© 2007 Mirage Studios, Inc.

© 2007 Mirage Studios, Inc.

© 2007 Mirage Studios, Inc.

© 2007 Mirage Studios, Inc.

© 2007 Mirage Studios, Inc.

© 2007 Mirage Studios, Inc.

Turtle Talk: Leonardo

Materials:
Crayons, markers, or paint
Scissors
Brown paper lunch bag
Glue

Instructions:

1. Color in the image on this page.
2. Carefully cut out the picture with an adult's help, and then cut it in half along the dashed lines.
3. Turn a brown paper lunch bag upside down. Leave it closed.
4. Glue the top of Leonardo's head to the flap of the bag.
5. Glue the bottom half of Leonardo's head to the front of the paper bag, right under the edge of the flap.
6. Stick your hand in the bag and place your fingers in the flap to make Leonardo talk!

© 2007 Mirage Studios, Inc.

© 2007 Mirage Studios, Inc.

© 2007 Mirage Studios, Inc.

© 2007 Mirage Studios, Inc.

© 2007 Mirage Studios, Inc.

© 2007 Mirage Studios, Inc.

© 2007 Mirage Studios, Inc.

© 2007 Mirage Studios, Inc.

© 2007 Mirage Studios, Inc.

© 2007 Mirage Studios, Inc.

© 2007 Mirage Studios, Inc.

© 2007 Mirage Studios, Inc.

© 2007 Mirage Studios, Inc.

© 2007 Mirage Studios, Inc.

© 2007 Mirage Studios, Inc.

© 2007 Mirage Studios, Inc.

© 2007 Mirage Studios, Inc.

© 2007 Mirage Studios, Inc.

© 2007 Mirage Studios, Inc.

© 2007 Mirage Studios, Inc.

© 2007 Mirage Studios, Inc.

© 2007 Mirage Studios, Inc.

© 2007 Mirage Studios, Inc.

© 2007 Mirage Studios, Inc.

© 2007 Mirage Studios, Inc.

© 2007 Mirage Studios, Inc.

© 2007 Mirage Studios, Inc.

© 2007 Mirage Studios, Inc.

Turtle Talk: Michelangelo

Materials:
Crayons, markers, or paint
Scissors
Brown paper lunch bag
Glue

Instructions:

1. Color in the image on this page.
2. Carefully cut out the picture with an adult's help, and then cut it in half along the dashed lines.
3. Turn a brown paper lunch bag upside down. Leave it closed.
4. Glue the top of Michelangelo's head to the flap of the bag.
5. Glue the bottom half of Michelangelo's head to the front of the paper bag, right under the edge of the flap.
6. Stick your hand in the bag and place your fingers in the flap to make Michelangelo talk!

43

© 2007 Mirage Studios, Inc.

© 2007 Mirage Studios, Inc.

© 2007 Mirage Studios, Inc.

© 2007 Mirage Studios, Inc.

© 2007 Mirage Studios, Inc.

© 2007 Mirage Studios, Inc.

© 2007 Mirage Studios, Inc.

© 2007 Mirage Studios, Inc.

© 2007 Mirage Studios, Inc.

© 2007 Mirage Studios, Inc.

© 2007 Mirage Studios, Inc.

© 2007 Mirage Studios, Inc.

© 2007 Mirage Studios, Inc.

© 2007 Mirage Studios, Inc.

© 2007 Mirage Studios, Inc.

© 2007 Mirage Studios, Inc.

© 2007 Mirage Studios, Inc.

© 2007 Mirage Studios, Inc.

© 2007 Mirage Studios, Inc.

© 2007 Mirage Studios, Inc.

© 2007 Mirage Studios, Inc.

© 2007 Mirage Studios, Inc.

© 2007 Mirage Studios, Inc.

© 2007 Mirage Studios, Inc.

© 2007 Mirage Studios, Inc.

© 2007 Mirage Studios, Inc.

© 2007 Mirage Studios, Inc.

© 2007 Mirage Studios, Inc.

Ninja Jumble

Unscramble the letters in each word, then write your answers on the lines below. When you're done, put the circled letters together to answer this question:

WHICH TURTLE IS THE LEADER?

C H O L E M I L A N G E

_ _ _ _ _ _(_)_ _ _(_)_(_)

T R I W E N S

_ _(_)_ _ _ _

P A H R L E A

_(_)_ _ _ _ _

R I P A L

_ _(_)_ _

L O O L A D N E T

(_)_ _ _ _ _ _ _(_)

JUMBLE ANSWER: _ _ _ _ _ _ _ _ _

Answers

Page 9

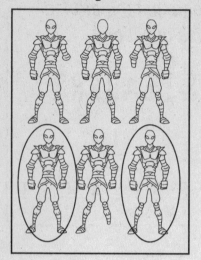

Page 10

MICHELANGELO

Page 13

Page 23

Page 25

1. APRIL

2. CASEY

3. SPLINTER

4. KARAI

Page 26

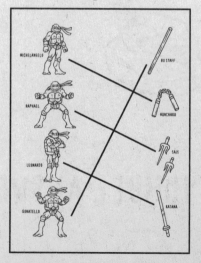

Answers

Page 27

COWABUNGA, DUDES!

Page 34

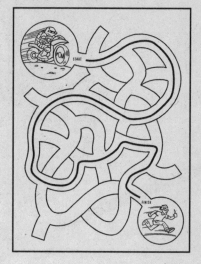

Page 37

19 18 1 13 10 9 11   18 11
 W I N T E R S   I S

23 2 3 13 24
 Y A O T L !

NINJA CODE KEY:

Page 38

ACROSS
1. THE TEENAGE MUTANT NINJA
   TURTLES' MASTER
2. THE TURTLES' BEST HUMAN FRIEND

DOWN
3. RAPHAEL'S WEAPONS OF CHOICE
4. GLOBAL NINJA CRIME ORGANIZATION
5. MICHELANGELO'S FAVORITE FOOD

Page 45

WHICH TURTLE IS THE LEADER?

CHOLEMILANGE
MICHE(L)ANG(E)L(O)

TR I WENS
WI(N)TERS

P A HRLEA
R(A)PHAEL

RI PAL
AP(R)LL

LOOLAUNE T
(O)ONATELL(O)

JUMBLE ANSWER: LEONARDO

47

TMNT
VIDEO GAME

Intense ninja action and amazing acrobatic moves!

Coming Spring 2007

 Visit www.esrb.org for updated rating information.

UBISOFT®

© 2007 Mirage Studios, Inc.